YORK NOTES

Hobson's Choice

Harold Brighouse

Notes by Brian Dyke

 Longman   York Press

YORK PRESS
322 Old Brompton Road, London SW5 9JH

ADDISON WESLEY LONGMAN LIMITED
Edinburgh Gate, Harlow,
Essex CM20 2JE, United Kingdom
Associated companies, branches and representatives throughout the world

First published 1997

ISBN 0–582–31352–X

Designed by Vicki Pacey, Trojan Horse
Illustrated by Chris Brown
Typeset by Pantek Arts, Maidstone, Kent
Phototypeset by Gem Graphics, Trenance, Mawgan Porth, Cornwall
Produced by Longman Asia Limited, Hong Kong
Colour reproduction and film output by Spectrum Colour

CONTENTS

PREFACE

York Notes are designed to give you a broader perspective on works of literature studied at GCSE and equivalent levels. We have carried out extensive research into the needs of the modern literature student prior to publishing this new edition. Our research showed that no existing series fully met students' requirements. Rather than present a single authoritative approach, we have provided alternative viewpoints, empowering students to reach their own interpretations of the text. York Notes provide a close examination of the work and include biographical and historical background, summaries, glossaries, analyses of characters, themes, structure and language, cultural connections and literary terms.

If you look at the Contents page you will see the structure for the series. However, there's no need to read from the beginning to the end as you would with a novel, play, poem or short story. Use the Notes in the way that suits you. Our aim is to help you with your understanding of the work, not to dictate how you should learn.

York Notes are written by English teachers and examiners, with an expert knowledge of the subject. They show you how to succeed in coursework and examination assignments, guiding you through the text and offering practical advice. Questions and comments will extend, test and reinforce your knowledge. Attractive colour design and illustrations improve clarity and understanding, making these Notes easy to use and handy for quick reference.

York Notes are ideal for:

- Essay writing
- Exam preparation
- Class discussion

The author of these Notes is Brian Dyke who has taught English since 1967 and has recently retired from his post of Head of English. He studied at St Luke's College, Exeter and gained a BA Degree from the Open University.

The text used in these Notes is the Heinemann edition, 1992.

Health Warning: **This study guide will enhance your understanding, but should not replace the reading of the original text and/or study in class.**

PART ONE

INTRODUCTION

HOW TO STUDY A PLAY

You have bought this book because you wanted to study a play on your own. This may supplement classwork.

- Drama is a special 'kind' of writing (the technical term is 'genre') because it needs a performance in the theatre to arrive at a full interpretation of its meaning. When reading a play you have to imagine how it should be performed; the words alone will not be sufficient. Think of gestures and movements.

- Drama is always about conflict of some sort (it may be below the surface). Identify the conflicts in the play and you will be close to identifying the large ideas or themes which bind all the parts together.

- Make careful notes on themes, characters, plot and any sub-plots of the play.

- Playwrights find non-realistic ways of allowing an audience to see into the minds and motives of their characters. The 'soliloquy', in which a character speaks directly to the audience, is one such device. Does the play you are studying have any such passages?

- Which characters do you like or dislike in the play? Why? Do your sympathies change as you see more of these characters?

- Think of the playwright writing the play. Why were these particular arrangements of events, these particular sets of characters and these particular speeches chosen?

Studying on your own requires self-discipline and a carefully thought-out work plan in order to be effective. Good luck.

Harold Brighouse was born in Eccles, Lancashire in 1882. He died in 1958. Harold Brighouse's father worked for the firm of Holdsworth and Gibb in the Manchester cotton business. His father was what we would now call a 'workaholic', he was also a magistrate and treasurer of the local Liberal Association. Thus, Harold Brighouse's background was comfortable without being luxurious. His mother had been a headmistress, and it is worth noting that Harold's father had previously been married to Harold's mother's sister which, at the time, rendered Harold and his sister illegitimate. To Harold Brighouse, this unconventional history of his parents, far from an embarrassment, 'asserted independence of mind' (see Harold Brighouse's autobiography, *What I Have Had*, 1953).

Harold Brighouse himself showed this 'independence of mind' in not fulfilling his mother's hopes for him of an academic career. He attended Manchester Grammar School, but left when he was 17, and went into the export side of the cotton business. He worked and studied hard at his career, but his passion was the theatre. Manchester was blessed with theatres and music halls and Harold Brighouse visited them as frequently as possible.

The beginning of Brighouse's involvement with 'theatre'

He moved to London when he was 20 and became an avid theatre-goer and 'first-nighter'. The Court Theatre (now the Royal Court) was run by Granville-Barker and was to be the centre of a revival in British Theatre. It broke from the tradition of basing productions around a 'star' performer and became responsible for the Repertory Movement, where plays and not personalities were important.

Harold Brighouse learnt the essence of his craft by theatre-going. Harold Brighouse married and returned to live in Manchester, but regularly visited London. On one of these visits, when watching what he considered to be a poor play, he decided he could do better, and he set about writing an unsuccessful five-act play. He had success with a one-act play *Lonesome-Like* in 1909 and from then on he made his living from writing. His first full-length play was *Dealing in Future* (1910) which dealt with the topic of workers in a chemical factory being poisoned by the dyes used in their works – thus set firmly in the Lancashire context.

Note the importance of the Lancashire context.

In 1907 Miss A.E. Horniman had established the Gaiety Theatre in Manchester, which became the centre of the Manchester School (see Literary Terms), of whom Harold Brighouse was the most successful. He wrote many one-act plays, fifteen full-length plays and eight novels. He wrote for the *Manchester Guardian* as theatre critic. Harold Brighouse gave up writing in 1930, but he wrote his autobiography, *What I Have Had*, in 1953.

Hobson's Choice (1916) outshines all his other works, and it is for *Hobson's Choice* that Harold Brighouse is remembered. It has remained a hugely popular play.

The origin of the phrase 'Hobson's choice' is in the practice of a seventeenth-century Cambridgeshire horse trader, Hobson, who offered customers a 'free choice' but in reality they had no choice at all, but always ended up with the horse that was available. Thus 'Hobson's choice' is no choice at all.

The way the play came to be written is interesting as the seed was sown at the Gaiety Theatre in Manchester. Harold Brighouse was discussing an actor's poor performance with his friends Ben Iden Payne and Stanley Houghton. Iden Payne said the choice of the actor had been Hobson's choice, there being no-one else available to take on the part. The three friends argued over Iden Payne's suggestion that Hobson's choice would be a good title for a play. On the toss of a coin it was agreed that Harold Brighouse should write the play. The idea therefore was conceived in the repertory tradition.

Hobson's Choice was born partly by chance and partly through the profound wartime experience of Brighouse.

Although the idea came from what seems a chance and flimsy beginning, the eventual circumstances that spurred Harold Brighouse to write the play could not have been more different. He was working in France in 1914, and on the outbreak of war he had to leave for England; France was conscripting its young men into their army and Harold Brighouse shared a traumatic bus journey to the port. The bus held three weeping women and men, all of whom were travelling to enlist in the French army. Harold Brighouse later wrote 'That bus collaborated with me in writing *Hobson's Choice*'.

Harold Brighouse was profoundly moved by the emotion he witnessed on the bus, by the 'choice' forced upon the men and women of a conscript nation. Stanley Houghton had died in 1913 and Harold Brighouse found himself with the emotional drive for his play. In his autobiography he wrote: 'Emotional experience is written off by an author in a form which may bear no resemblance to the originating disturbance.' So Harold Brighouse had his muse (see Literary Terms). He wrote 'I was a writer with an emotional load to get rid of, and at a sharp tangent to the bus to Havre I recollected Salford, where in Cross Lane my father was born, and I wrote *Hobson's Choice.*'

Social background

Having had a clue to Harold Brighouse's emotion in writing the play, we can consider the emotions that are explained in the play, and we must remember that the audience of at this time lived in a very different society from our own. The play has much to say about love, conflict and ambition. It is Maggie who has the power for change, and at this time women were fighting hard to achieve a fairer society. Women's emancipation strikes a chord today, and in 1916 social problems were at the heart of much theatre of the day. The infamous 'Cat and Mouse Act' was brought into force in 1913 when suffragette disorder had reached its height; women in Britain were still unable to vote in national elections at the outbreak of the First World War, and a woman's property was in law her husband's property. Harold Brighouse set the play in 1870 but the themes of the right of women to determine their own lives and the rebellion of the younger generation against parental tyranny were current when it was first performed.

The role of women in society had been treated by Ibsen, and the theme was taken up by George Bernard Shaw. Shaw wrote eight major plays between 1900 and 1914; all had a strong social or political message. The tormented Swedish dramatist August Strindberg examined the institution of marriage in *The Dance of Death* (1901). Anton Chekhov was another giant of the theatre. His plays have an atmosphere of humour and pathos, his characters are ordinary people rather than heroes or villains. Shaw wrote his plays trying to drive home a message, H.G. Wells wrote science fiction and

Although a product of its time, Hobson's Choice speaks to all generations; its universality is evident.

social and comic novels. It is worth reading *Kipps* and *The History of Mr Polly*. *Hobson's Choice* is set in Lancashire, and indeed this is an important facet of the play, it has a universality (see Literary Terms) which makes it valid for people everywhere. The comments on the relationships of the professions, business and trade are firmly a period comment but the attitudes surrounding those comments, the ideas of love, conflict and improvement are undated, and perhaps the treatment of 'class' has a particular relevance to British audiences. Although the play was a product of its time it has transcended historical limits. Interestingly, the fall of Hobson conforms to the traditions of classical comedy where a main character incurs the disapproval of the audience because of his behaviour. Hobson is debunked and laughed at while Maggie sets the standards of desirable behaviour, and although Hobson is a fallen character (see Literary Terms), Maggie encourages sympathy for him at the end. We can say that our play combines the best of classical literature with its treatment of theme (see Literary Terms), and modern literature with its treatment of character. It is a recipe likely to ensure continuing popularity.

PART TWO

SUMMARIES

GENERAL SUMMARY

Act I	Alice, Vickey and Maggie are in the shop when Albert Prosser enters to court Alice; apart from Maggie they are clearly in fear of their father, Hobson, who is recovering from his previous night's drinking. Maggie forces Albert to buy boots and laces and Alice complains she is an 'old maid'. Hobson enters and lectures his daughters on 'uppishness'. He feels they are trying to control him. He complains of the 'bustles' Alice and Vickey have worn in public and gives them their ultimatum; they will behave as he wants them to, or he will marry them off.
Maggie says nothing while Mrs Hepworth speaks to Willie, but can we speculate on her thoughts.	As Hobson is about to leave, Mrs Hepworth enters. She is searching for Willie, Hobson's bootmaker, who has made the best boots she has ever worn. We learn that Willie can scarcely read. Hobson is obsequious towards Mrs Hepworth, but as soon as she leaves he resumes his domineering attitude.
	Jim Heeler calls on Hobson to take him to 'Moonraker's'. Hobson seeks his advice on managing his daughters. Heeler's final solution is to 'get 'em wed'. Hobson's plan is to keep Maggie at home, but to marry off Alice and Vickey. But when Heeler says that the two marriages will cost Hobson, he rejects the idea of weddings.
	Maggie tells Willie he is a genius at bootmaking and wants to know his ambitions. Will acknowledges Maggie's brilliance in managing the shop, and then Maggie proposes marriage to Will. Will is 'tokened' to Ada Figgins but Maggie makes it clear to Ada that she is claiming Will. Maggie instructs Will to arrange for the banns to be called.

Maggie informs Alice and Vickey of her intentions and
they are horrified. Hobson returns and Maggie tells
him the news. Hobson is against the match but Maggie
holds her course. Hobson calls Will to the shop with
the intention of beating the love from him with his
belt. When Hobson strikes him, Will kisses Maggie
and is ready to leave with her immediately if Hobson
strikes again. Hobson stands amazed and undecided
what to do.

Act II

*Note the
importance of the
'Moonraker's' in
Hobson's
deterioration.*

It is a month later, Maggie and Will have taken
premises in Oldfield Road. Hobson is spending more
and more time at 'Moonraker's'. Alice and Vickey are
unable to manage the business. Maggie is executing her
plan to effect the marriages of Alice and Vickey. Will
and Maggie are to be married this day, while Hobson is
sleeping and 'trespassing' in the Beenstock Warehouse.
Hobson is issued with a writ for trespassing, damage
and spying. The 'fine' to keep the case out of court will
give Alice and Vickey the capital to start their
marriages.

Act III

Maggie and Will are entertaining Vickey and her
boyfriend, Freddie Beenstock, and Alice and Albert to
their wedding feast in the cellar at Oldfield Road.
Hobson arrives to ask Maggie for help in dealing with
the writ. Hobson is terrified of the publicity a court
action will attract. Albert presses the case to Hobson
who eventually asks 'how much' to keep quiet – £500 is
agreed. When Hobson understands that the money will
be used to set up Alice and Vickey in marriages, he
storms out, disowning his daughters and predicting a
bleak future for his daughters' husbands. When Will is
left alone with Maggie we see his trepidation and it is
left to Maggie to lead him to the bedroom.

Act IV

It is a year later and Hobson has had a breakdown. Tubby is housekeeping for Hobson – there is little to do in the workshop since the business is failing. Jim Heeler listens to Hobson's symptoms – alcoholism is clearly the cause. When Doctor MacFarlane calls, he insists that Hobson stops drinking and has Maggie back to look after him.

Maggie makes it clear that she would not choose to return to Hobson, and the decision must be Will's. Alice and Vickey both recoil at the idea of looking after Hobson, and consider it is Maggie's duty to do so.

Note the great change that has taken place in Will.

When Will arrives he immediately inspects the stock. Alice and Vickey fear that they will lose their inheritances, but Will makes it clear that the business has declined so that it is worth little. Hobson tries to dictate terms to Maggie and Will until it is obvious that Will and Maggie will leave for their own prosperous business which has taken Hobson's trade.

Will makes his offer to Hobson; he will return with Hobson playing no active part in the business and on the condition that the shop is called 'Mossop's'. Maggie tempers Will's condition by having the shop renamed 'Mossop & Hobson'. Will immediately plans expensive alterations and tells Maggie to take Hobson to draw up legalities. Hobson is crushed and Will is seen to be confident and able. The transformation is complete.

ACT I

Act I opens with Hobson's younger daughters in the 'dingy but business-like' boot shop. Alice is twenty-three and Victoria (always referred to as Vickey) is twenty-one and very pretty. Hobson's eldest daughter enters; Maggie is thirty and she is immediately busy with an accounts book when she sits at her desk.

We see Alice's and Vickey's fear of their father.

We have our first hint of Hobson's drinking habits.

We learn that Hobson is late having been to a Mason's meeting the previous night. Alice is expecting Albert Prosser to visit the shop. She wishes Hobson would go out to leave the shop free for her to entertain Albert and for her sisters to go into the house. We learn that Hobson, far from having breakfast, will need reviving!

Albert Prosser enters the shop. He is twenty-six, the son of a 'prosperous solicitor' and is courting Alice. He turns to go when he learns that Hobson is still at home, but Maggie stops him. She is 'sick of the sight of him' and proceeds to teach Albert and Alice a lesson. Maggie asks Albert 'what can we do for you Mr Prosser' and makes it clear that she wishes him to buy something. Albert tries to escape with buying only bootlaces but Maggie 'pushes him' to sit down and takes off one of his boots. Vickey brings a pair of size eight boots and Maggie fits one on him and laces it. Alice and Albert both protest but Maggie overrules them and Albert can only complain that he merely wanted bootlaces. Albert is billed for repairs to his old boots as well as the new ones.

Note the humour surrounding the 'braid' and 'leather' laces.

Hobson, wearing a Masonic chain, comes into the shop and announces he is going out 'for a quarter of an hour'. Maggie knows that he will be going to Moonraker's and tells him not to be late for dinner. Hobson uses a chair to face all of them and complain about interference. Hobson brushes aside Maggie's reminder that Jim Heeler will be waiting and lectures his daughters.

What is Maggie's point here?

Vickey and Alice complain that they are not bumptious and Vickey asks for 'give and take'. When Hobson retorts, 'I give and you take', Maggie raises a central issue. She asks, 'How much a week do you give us?' Hobson brushes this aside and continues his tirade against 'uppishness'. He warns his daughters that their 'conduct' must change. Hobson says he has been disgusted by the way Alice and Vickey dress.

Hobson complains about the 'bustles' worn by Alice and Vickey. He pays Tudsbury £10 a year to dress the girls which 'pleases the eye and is good for trade'. Hobson is outraged by the 'hump added to nature behind you'. He complains that the wagging hump is 'immodest'. Hobson feels that the new fashion is against his 'common-sense and sincerity'. Hobson is 'British middle-class and proud of it!'.

Note the humour when Alice remonstrates, 'can't we choose husbands for ourselves'.

When the girls refuse 'to dress like mill girls' Hobson gives them an ultimatum: they will control their uppishness or he will choose husbands for them. When Maggie asks about a husband for her, Hobson ridicules her as being past the marrying age and a proper old maid. When Maggie states she is thirty, Hobson cruelly replies, 'Aye, thirty and shelved'.

Mrs Hepworth enters and wants to know who made the boots she is wearing. She is well-dressed with a curt manner, Hobson makes himself ridiculous as he kneels and fondles her boots. Hobson assumes something is wrong with the boots. Maggie calls Tubby Wadlow from the workshop below. Tubby says that Willie Mossop made the boots and Willie is summoned.

Willie thinks Mrs Hepworth is about to strike him but she hands in her visiting card which he cannot read. Hobson assumes there is a problem but Mrs Hepworth explains that the boots Willie made for her are the best she has ever had and that Willie must make her boots in future, and inform her if he moves from Hobson's.

When Hobson declares 'he won't change', Mrs Hepworth praises Willie to Hobson's discomfiture – 'The man's a treasure and I expect you underpay him?'

What does this tell us about Will's frame of mind?

Willie, to his great relief, dives down the trap 'like a rabbit'.

Mrs Hepworth declares that she will have only Will to make boots for herself and her daughters. Once Mrs Hepworth has left Hobson's, he resumes his domineering attitude, complaining that Mrs Hepworth's praise will make the workmen 'uppish'.

Hobson's friend, the grocer Jim Heeler, calls to take Hobson to Moonraker's, but Hobson surprises everyone by refusing the invitation. He wants 'private' talk with Jim Heeler. Hobson wants advice from Heeler on how to manage his daughters, or escape the 'dominion' of three women.

Choose your 'favourite' comment.

Jim agrees that Hobson is a fine talker but Hobson complains his daughters think him a 'wind-bag'. Hobson and Heeler exchange chauvinist comments about the 'foolishness' of women. When Hobson says he has tried all methods of controlling his daughters and he is 'fair moithered', Jim gives his solution – 'Quit roaring at 'em and get 'em wed'.

Why does he want 'temperance young men'?

Hobson says the difficulty is finding 'temperance young men' and when Heeler says that would be too difficult for *three* daughters, Hobson reveals his plan: 'Maggie's too useful to part with' and 'a bit on the ripe side for marrying'. Hobson says that if he marries off one daughter his problem will be solved: 'Get one wedding in a family and it goes through the lot like measles'.

Jim then mentions settlements – 'It'll cost you a bit you know' and Hobson changes his mind – 'I'd a fancy for a bit of peace, but there's luxuries a man can buy too dear' – and then goes to 'Moonraker's'.

What reasons would you give for his reluctance?

Maggie summons Willie who comes from the trap 'reluctantly'. Maggie holds and 'retains' Willie's hands. Will states that 'they're dirty' but Maggie's interest is that 'they're clever'. Maggie claims that Will is 'a natural born genius at making boots. It's a pity you're a natural fool at all else.'

Willie agrees he is no use with anything but leather and is surprised when Maggie asks 'when are you going to leave Hobson's?' Will states that he is a 'loyal fool' and Maggie asks her central question: 'Don't you want to get on, Will Mossop?' Maggie tells Will he could earn much more in 'one of the big shops in Manchester'. He says he would be 'feared' to go. And Maggie wants to know what keeps him – 'Is it the – the people?'

Why is this so important a question in relation to the whole play?

Maggie tells Will that the success of Hobson's is due to his good workmanship and her persuasive ability to sell. Maggie uses her authority to keep Will from going down his 'trap' and comes to her point. She tells him that she has counted on him for six months and that she wants to invest in him – her brain and his hands will make a working partnership. Will is relieved: 'Partnership! Oh that's a different thing. I thought you were axing me to wed you.' But then Maggie says that she is! Will recognises Maggie's attributes but plainly tells her, 'I'm none in love with you'. Maggie shows not only her resolution to achieve 'the best we can get out of it' but also her feelings: 'I've got the love all right'.

Will is frightened of Hobson's reactions and reveals that he 'is tokened to Ada Figgins', his landlady's daughter, and Ada will soon arrive with his lunch. Maggie is disparaging of Ada and shows that she will let nothing stand in her way. She tells Will that if he gives his 'helpless' Ada the 'protection' she craves he will 'be an eighteen shilling a week bootmaker all the days of your life' and a 'contented slave'. When Willie protests he is not ambitious, Maggie makes it clear he is 'going to be' and with her spider-fly image (see Literary Terms) declares 'You're my man, Willie Mossop'.

Ada meekly enters with Willie's dinner and Maggie bars her exit. Ada tells Maggie that Willie plays his Jew's harp well and that he is 'the lad I love'. Maggie astonishes Ada with 'I can say the same'. When Ada cannot offer her ideas for Willie's future, Maggie claims him and Willie feels 'there's no escape'.

Maggie dismisses Ada from the shop and Ada threatens Will with her mother's wrath. Maggie immediately decides that Will should not return to Mrs Figgins's house and that Tubby Wadlow will collect Will's things. Will is immensely relieved to be released from Ada's clutches: 'It's like an 'appy dream. Eh, Maggie, you do manage things.'

Will 'kissing' is significant a number of times in the play. Look out for them.

Maggie instructs Will to arrange for the banns to be called that evening and then tells him to kiss her. Will is taken aback – 'It's like saying I agree to everything a kiss is'. Will is holding out against the kiss when Alice and Vickey enter and he 'dives for the trap' and escapes the situation.

Maggie announces her intention to Alice and Vickey in a totally matter-of-fact manner. Alice and Vickey are

How does Maggie say Albert must change?

amazed and mortified. Alice feels the 'disgrace' keenly and feels it will spoil her chances with Albert. Maggie states that Alice will marry Albert when he is more responsible.

Hobson returns and is belligerent about dinner not being ready. Vickey raises the subject of the 'news' and Alice asks him if he would like Will 'in the family'. Maggie tells Hobson plainly she is to marry Will – she is *not* 'past the marrying age'. To the consternation of Alice and Vickey, Hobson states, 'I'll have no husbands here!' and 'There'll be no weddings here'. He demands his dinner but Maggie stands up to him as Alice and Vickey protest as they are driven into the kitchen.

Compare this to Maggie's statements to Will about fools on page 15.

This time Maggie says, 'I'm not a fool and you're not a fool', but Hobson is adamant that she can't have Will and that 'His father was a work-house brat'.

Maggie overrides Hobson's protests and states her terms – Will will be paid the same wages and she will work eight hours a day for 15 shillings a week.

Hobson complains he is not 'made of brass' and Maggie retorts that if she and Will leave, Hobson will be unable to spend time at Moonraker's, as he will be having to 'watch all day' cheap 'shop hands'.

Hobson removes his belt and calls Will from the workshop. Hobson threatens Will who appeals to Maggie who responds, 'I'm watching you my lad'. Hobson allows that Willie can keep his job but threatens 'we must beat love from your body' as he prepares to strike Will. Will claims that Hobson is making a great mistake but Hobson continues to swing the strap. Willie continues that he will 'take her quick, aye, and stick to her like glue' if Hobson strikes him. Hobson strikes Will who then kisses Maggie and claims that if 'Hobson raises that strap again, I'll do more. I'll walk straight out of shop with thee and us two 'ull set up for ourselves'.

Will seems drained of action after this. Maggie resumes control as she 'puts her arm round his neck'. She rejoices 'Willie! I knew you had it in you, lad'.

Hobson stands in amazed indecision! He could never have envisaged Willie's reaction.

COMMENT

Maggie shows her disapproval of Alice's and Albert's 'courting'. Her treatment of Albert Prosser gives an early indication of her strength of character, and shows the agility of her mind – Albert is billed for repairs to his old boots as well as the new ones.

At the very start of the play we see seeds of Hobson's downfall – his drinking. It is expected that he will return to Moonraker's for 'reviving'.

What does Jim Heeler think about Hobson's treatment of his daughters?

Hobson controls his daughters – he pays his draper £10 a year to dress them 'proper', but pays them no wages – as he says to Heeler, 'I'm not a fool' (p. 14). He calls them 'rebellious females of this house', and that it has been 'coming on ever since your mother died'. He complains about their 'uppishness' and claims that 'you'll none rule me'. However, we see that Maggie can stand up to Hobson when she reminds him that dinner is at one o'clock (p. 14). We also see that she is reasonable and understanding when she says 'we'll give him half an hour'.

Mrs Hepworth's visit is crucial to the events of the play and reveals an important aspect of Hobson's character (see Literary Terms).

The conversation between Hobson and Jim Heeler reveals much of the accepted relationships between men and women of the time.

Maggie has seen potential in Will and 'counted on' him for six months. There is an irony (see Literary Terms) as the serious and practical Maggie is spurred into action when Hobson reacts to Alice's and Vickey's wearing of 'bustles'. Note that Maggie shows some emotion when she asks Will what keeps him at Hobson's (p. 15).

Hobson has revealed his hatred of lawyers when he states that he hates bumptiousness like he hates a lawyer (p. 5).

GLOSSARY

masons a 'secret society' exclusive to men

the hump was wagging the hump is a bustle, fashionable at the time and 'wagging' suggests a flirtatious walk

temperance young men young men who don't drink alcohol

settlements money given to 'marry off' a daughter

axing asking

by gum an expression of astonishment

a Salford life's too near the bone too difficult to bear

tokened promised, engaged

you're treading on my foot you're in my way

she'll jaw me she'll give me a piece of her mind

a come-by-chance born out of wedlock

settle my life's course decide my future

John Bright English statesman and famous orator (1811–89)

moithered muddled, confused

Identify the speaker.

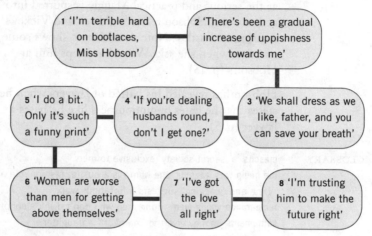

1 'I'm terrible hard on bootlaces, Miss Hobson'

2 'There's been a gradual increase of uppishness towards me'

5 'I do a bit. Only it's such a funny print'

4 'If you're dealing husbands round, don't I get one?'

3 'We shall dress as we like, father, and you can save your breath'

6 'Women are worse than men for getting above themselves'

7 'I've got the love all right'

8 'I'm trusting him to make the future right'

Check your answers on page 67.

Consider these issues.

a The significance of Albert Prosser's visit to the shop.

b The reasons behind Hobson's disapproval of bustles.

c How Maggie's relationships with Hobson is different from Vickey's and Alice's relationships with Hobson.

d The importance of Mrs Hepworth's visit to the shop.

e The significance of Ada's appearance in Act I.

f The way Will Mossop changes in Act I.

It is a month later. The setting is the same as in Act I, but Alice is in Maggie's chair, Vickey is reading and Tubby Wadlow is waiting for instructions. There is nothing in the workshop which needs doing, 'We're worked up' complains Tubby. We learn that 'The high-class trade has dropped like a stone'.

Note the humour of Alice and Vickey being unable to add simple figures.

Hobson is not in and Tubby is nervous of his temper when he returns. We see discord and indecision: Vickey and Alice are unable to make business decisions. Tubby unhappily returns to the workshop to make clogs, and we learn that Hobson is 'wasting more time than ever in the Moonraker's'.

Both girls wish they were 'married and out of it'. Alice is surprised at Vickey's admission and Vickey pointedly says 'Nobody's fretting to get Willie Mossop for a brother-in-law'. Maggie and Freddie arrive and she squashes the complaints of Alice and Vickey that their chances of marriage are hindered by Maggie's engagement to Will. She despatches Freddie to bring Albert Prosser to the shop. When Alice voices the worry that Hobson might return she is told that Hobson is 'sleeping' in the cellar of Freddie Beenstock's corn warehouse, safely snoring having fallen 'soft on some bags'.

Maggie is taking control of events.

Maggie makes it clear that she is about to arrange marriages for Alice and Vickey, and she insists that her sisters treat Willie as part of the family: 'If you want your Freddie, and if you want your Albert, you'll be respectful to my Willie.' Maggie insists that Alice and Vickey kiss their 'brother-in-law to be'. First Vickey kisses Will 'under protest' and Will 'rather likes it' then Alice follows.

The sisters have 'approved' Will with their kisses.

Maggie is obviously amazed that Hobson has put Alice in charge of accounting and refuses to help Alice with the books. Maggie insists that Alice and Vickey leave the shop to attend her wedding with Will, and the 'wedding spread' later that night.

We see the different values of Maggie compared with Alice and Vickey. Hobson is 'safe where he is' and Tubby is to be left to 'see to the shop'. Maggie buys a brass ring for her wedding finger, to the astonishment of Alice and Vickey. They make it clear that they would be satisfied only with the best and Maggie 'tricks' them out of furniture from the lumber room. Although it is broken, 'Will's handy with his fingers'. Alice and Vickey start to think that the furniture is too good for them to lose, but Maggie tells them it is in exchange for their 'marriage portions'.

Alice and Vickey are herded out to dress for the wedding. Freddie returns with Albert to produce his 'blue paper'. The paper, in legal jargon, is 'far from good law' but is a writ against Hobson for trespass, damage and spying on the premises of Jonathan Beenstock and Co. (where he is currently 'sleeping').

Freddie is despatched to put the paper on Hobson. Albert accepts that he must follow Maggie's instruction, much to his chagrin, to push the handcart containing the furniture to '39a, Oldfield Road' while Maggie, Will, Alice and Vickey go to the Church.

What is the joke about 'church' and 'the dentist's'?

Maggie asks Will for his feelings, and we learn from Willie that 'you're growing on me lass'. Willie is 'resigned' and states he will 'toe the line' with Maggie. Maggie takes charge of the ring!

COMMENT

Will and Maggie have clearly taken away the high-class trade from Hobson; Hobson has lost the boot-making skills of Willie and the management skills of Maggie. Without Maggie, business is deteriorating.

Hobson is clearly spending more time drinking at 'Moonraker's' and is losing touch with his business.

Maggie is prepared to use her devious scheme in promoting her ambition and arranging the three marriages. We see that she knows clearly what she is aiming at and that she 'don't allow folks to change their minds'. Another side of her character (see Literary Terms) is hinted at when she says that she's noticed that Will is 'no great hand at kissing'.

We clearly see the differences in outlook between Maggie and her sisters in relation to people and possessions.

Will's importance and esteem are bolstered by Maggie while Freddie and Albert are made to eat humble pie. Maggie's intention is to raise Will in his own eyes as well as her sisters' eyes – 'He's as good as you are now, and better'. She produces Will's business card and shows him to be his 'own master'.

The writ strikes at Hobson's weak spot and we see Maggie using her knowledge of Hobson's hatred of lawyers (Act I). Maggie knows that the action will not 'come to court'.

GLOSSARY   **play old Harry** be very angry
             nowty bad and variable
             all at sixes and sevens totally disorganised
             blood man of fashion
             I'd just as lief I'd just as soon
             Flat Iron Market second-hand market
             marriage portions dowries
             sithee look here
             throws old shoes good-luck custom for a wedding couple

A

Identify the speaker.

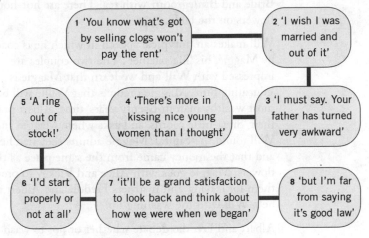

1 'You know what's got by selling clogs won't pay the rent'

2 'I wish I was married and out of it'

5 'A ring out of stock!'

4 'There's more in kissing nice young women than I thought'

3 'I must say. Your father has turned very awkward'

6 'I'd start properly or not at all'

7 'it'll be a grand satisfaction to look back and think about how we were when we began'

8 'but I'm far from saying it's good law'

Check your answers on page 67.

B

Consider these issues.

a The way Hobson's shop has changed since Will and Maggie left.

b What we gather of the way Hobson has been acting.

c The importance of Alice and Vickey kissing Will.

d What we learn from Maggie's choice of wedding ring.

e How Maggie intends to secure the 'marriage portions'.

f The purpose of Maggie insisting Albert pushes 'a hand-cart through Salford in broad daylight'.

g Maggie's and Will's feelings as they go to the church.

It is the wedding-night in the cellar at Oldfield Road. Albert and Alice, Vickey and Freddie are toasting 'The Bride and Bridegroom' with tea! There are hot-house flowers on the table.

Will makes an untypical speech in which he is coached by Maggie, his 'life partner'. The two couples are impressed with Will and we learn that Maggie is 'educating him'. Maggie predicts that Willie will be the most wealthy man in twenty years' time. Albert praises their 'Snug little rooms' and asks where Maggie and Will found the capital. Maggie admits they had help and that the money came from the same place as the flowers. Maggie goes with Alice and Vickey to prepare them for leaving and instructs Freddie and Albert to help Will with the washing up.

Albert and Freddie debate whether or not to wash up. They don't like the idea, but realise that Maggie needs to be 'kept the sweet side of' until the marriages have taken place. Will prepares the table for his 'schooling' but is anxious that Albert and Freddie do not go.

Maggie is raising Willie in Hobson's eyes.

Maggie returns as Hobson knocks at the door to the 'terror' of Vickey. Maggie ushers the two couples into the bedroom making it clear they must emerge to meet Hobson. Hobson makes to enter but Maggie tells him she must 'ask the Master' if she can let Hobson in.

Hobson is 'worse for wear' but Maggie insists that he eats some wedding cake. Having satisfied Maggie's wishes, Hobson explains his predicament, 'I'm in sore trouble, Maggie'.

Maggie makes it clear that nothing can be private from Will. 'Will and me's one.'

She makes Hobson tell his story to Will, 'man to man with no fools of women about'. Hobson produces the 'blue paper' which Maggie immediately hands to Will. Hobson blames Maggie for the writ, saying his visit to Moonraker's was to help him forget his 'thankless child', and he has awoken to 'lawyers … law-costs … publicity … ruin'. Hobson feels that he has fallen into the 'grip' of his 'hated lawyers'.

Hobson's disgrace is in being 'overcome at 12 o'clock in the morning' and he realises it will ruin his business when the affair appears not only in the *Salford Reporter* but also the *Manchester Guardian*. Willie unintentionally 'rubs salt into Hobson's wound', without 'malicious intention', and Hobson cannot contain his anger at Will's 'well-meant words'. Maggie quells Hobson as he starts to abuse Will. Hobson is most afraid of appearing in court where a lawyer will 'squeeze him where his squirming's seen the most'. Maggie suggests it could be settled 'in private' but Hobson fears that would 'cost a fortune', unless it was settled out of a lawyer's office.

Note the humour of Hobson's 'At your age'.

Maggie then plays her master stroke and to Hobson's amazement she calls Albert into the room. Alice, Vickey and Freddie then come from the bedroom. Hobson is enraged that Alice and Vickey have left Tubby to look after the shop, but Maggie explains that it was for her wedding day, and that Willie and she will do the same for Alice and Vickey on their wedding days. Hobson is adamant that there will be no more weddings – 'One daughter defying me is quite enough'.

Albert starts the 'business' and points out that Hobson's remarks could add 'libel' to the counts of 'trespass' and 'spying'. Hobson's 'you blood-sucking' simply spurs Albert to remind him that such insults may be 'remembered in the costs'. Hobson cuts through the preliminaries with 'How much? … What's the figure?'

Albert asks for a thousand pounds and, warming to his task, suggests an addition for saved 'doctor's bills'. Maggie states that Hobson can afford and will pay five hundred pounds. Hobson agrees to pay the money but reminds Vickey that it 'is a tidy bit of money to be going out of the family'. When Maggie explains that the money will be used for the weddings, Alice and Albert, Vickey and Freddie stand arm in arm, and the plan is revealed. Hobson is furious, 'I've been diddled. It's a plant'.

Note that Vickey complains that Hobson had not paid his daughters any wages.

Hobson feels he has been robbed. He makes it clear that he will run his business with men, and his daughters will not be welcome at home. 'I'm rid of ye, and it's a lasting riddance.' Hobson is stung over the money and angrily points out that Freddie's and Albert's responsibilities will be onerous. Hobson acknowledges Will's ability but counters that Albert is 'good at robbery'. He is full of bitterness and claims he will give the couples no future help – 'Wait till the families begin to come. Don't come to me for keep, that's all.'

The couples prepare to leave – to Will's disappointment: 'I wouldn't dream of asking you to go.' When Maggie and Will are alone, Maggie underlines her ambition to Will that he will grow to be more important than either Albert or Freddie. Maggie is teaching Will with a slate and slate pencil and will help bring about his advancement.

Maggie goes to the bedroom and Will is in an agony of indecision. Will is clearly frightened of entering the

bedroom. He decides to lie on the sofa, but with lovely symbolism (see Literary Terms) Maggie 'takes' him by the ear, and returns with him to the bedroom.

COMMENT   At the start of the act it is clear that Maggie is schooling Will – his speech has obviously been learnt.

Maggie and Will have had financial help in setting up their business – we learn that this help, and the flowers, come from Mrs Hepworth.

Will has not lost his fear of Maggie although he has willingly married her. He is afraid to be left alone with Maggie – 'I freely own I'm feeling awkward like'.

Will's attitude towards Hobson is an extension on Maggie's schooling although he has no intention of enraging Hobson. Note that Will plays no part in the negotiations with Albert and Freddie.

Hobson's hatred and fear of lawyers is clearly demonstrated.

Maggie is in control of people and events throughout the act and has clearly charted Will's future. We see her powers of management when she briefly introduces the idea of a counter-claim for 'personal damages'. However, we also see Maggie's sentimental side when she saves one of the flowers to press as a keepsake.

Hobson's decisions at the end of the meeting hold the seeds of his downfall; he will go to Moonraker's and staff his shop with men.

GLOSSARY   **gaffer** the boss
Salford Reporter local newspaper
Manchester Guardian a local daily paper which grew to national status (The *Guardian*)
cock-a-hooping cocky
diddled tricked
lumber up clutter up
sweet time (ironically) dreadful

A · Identify the speaker.

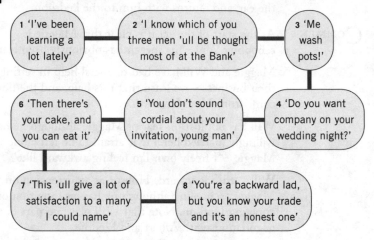

1 'I've been learning a lot lately'

2 'I know which of you three men 'ull be thought most of at the Bank'

3 'Me wash pots!'

6 'Then there's your cake, and you can eat it'

5 'You don't sound cordial about your invitation, young man'

4 'Do you want company on your wedding night?'

7 'This 'ull give a lot of satisfaction to a many I could name'

8 'You're a backward lad, but you know your trade and it's an honest one'

Check your answers on page 67.

B · Consider these issues.

a Why Will is keen for Albert and Freddie to stay.

b The part Will plays in Hobson's visit.

c The reasons for Maggie insisting Hobson eats wedding cake.

d The way Maggie manages the 'negotiations'.

e Why Hobson is so angry as he leaves.

f The way Maggie's character (see Literary Terms) is revealed in the act.

Y

ACT IV

We see that Tubby has nothing to do but keep house.

Act IV opens in Hobson's living-room, a year later. It is eight in the morning, and Tubby is 'incompetently' preparing a cooked breakfast. Hobson has said he is 'very ill' and sent Tubby to call Doctor MacFarlane and Jim Heeler. Heeler wants to go up to Hobson but we learn he is 'short-tempered this morning'. Tubby tells Jim Heeler that 'Mr Hobson's not his own self and the shop's not its own self.' We learn that clogs are the only line wanted in the shop. All the high-class trade has gone.

Tubby is proudly 'sticking to' Hobson, but he tells Heeler that 'Temper and obstinacy' are ruining the shop. Jim Heeler states that it is accepted that Willie Mossop has been the cause of Hobson's downfall, but Tubby honestly states that Hobson's lack of 'care ... and tact' prevented the shop from recovering from Willie's competition. Maggie had been the selling-force at Hobson's and Hobson has replaced his daughters with expensive 'men assistants'.

Tubby clearly sees the folly of not having women assistants in the shop.

Hobson enters unshaven, and speaks with 'acute melancholy and self-pity'. Jim Heeler tells Hobson he needs 'a woman about the house'. Tubby is desperate to fetch Maggie. Hobson rails against his daughters who have 'deserted' him, but pronounces himself a 'dying man' and then relents with 'go for her. Go for the Devil'.

Tubby goes and Hobson tells Jim that he is frightened of himself and is afraid of committing suicide. Hobson feels he is 'all one symptom, head to foot', and he is clear about the cause: Moonraker's. Jim Heeler is clearly afraid he might be in the same predicament.

Doctor MacFarlane enters, 'a domineering Scotsman of fifty'. The doctor is not pleased to be troubled by a patient well enough to be out of bed – he has been 'up

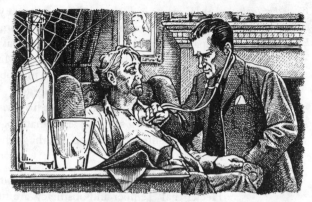

all night'. Jim Heeler is mistaken for the patient and pronounced to be in much the same condition. Doctor MacFarlane tells Hobson his condition is obvious to all but himself. To Hobson's complaint Doctor MacFarlane states 'Your complaint and your character are the same'. When Doctor MacFarlane makes to leave, Jim Heeler protests 'you have not diagnosed'. Heeler is told that if he is to remain he can 'keep his mouth shut'. To Heeler's disappointment, Hobson chooses that Doctor MacFarlane remains and Jim shall go. Doctor MacFarlane diagnoses a 'breakdown' and 'chronic alcoholism!'

Doctor MacFarlane threatens Hobson with certification and warns him 'you've drunk yourself within six months of the grave'. He prescribes a mixture and 'total abstinence'. Hobson is not inclined to 'lengthen out my unalcoholic days' and argues that 'life's got to be worth living before I'll live it'.

What does Hobson call his alcohol intake?

Hobson offers to pay for the Doctor's services and says that he is fortified to go again to 'Moonraker's'. Doctor MacFarlane refuses to go. Hobson is stated to be a 'pig-headed animal' to whom 'alcohol is poison'. Doctor MacFarlane is determined Hobson will 'die sober', and

asks Hobson if he has a wife. He states that Hobson
needs a woman to 'keep her thumb firm on ye'. He
states 'women are a necessity'. When Hobson says that
Maggie grew 'the worst of all', Doctor MacFarlane
insists that she returns to look after him – 'I prescribe
her!' As Hobson tries to argue the point Maggie enters
the room, having been fetched by Tubby, and Hobson
retaliates that Tubby will be 'sacked'.

What three
prescriptions does
Dr MacFarlane
leave?

Maggie is told that Hobson is 'drinking himself to
death' and that he can only be saved if Maggie comes
back to live with him. Hobson is disparaging about the
'sacrifice' Maggie would have to make by leaving her
'two cellars in Oldfield Road'. Maggie states that she
'might' but when pressed by Doctor MacFarlane she
exerts her control, to Hobson's pleasure, with 'The rest's
my business'. Doctor MacFarlane leaves in the 'profound
conviction' that Hobson is 'in excellent hands'.

Immediately, Maggie sends Tubby to collect the
prescribed 'mixture' and to 'tell Mr Mossop that I want
him quick!' Hobson tells Maggie he could not give up
alcohol, but Maggie counters that he could if she were
'here to make you' but first she must ask Will. Hobson
ridicules asking Will as a 'matter of form'. Maggie
makes it clear she would not choose to return to
Hobson but would do so out of duty. As Hobson tries
to exert his claims on Maggie, Alice enters, 'elaborately
dressed' and acting with a superior manner. She clearly
was still in bed when Tubby had called, unlike the 'wife
of a working cobbler'. Alice continues her haughty
manner both toward Maggie and Hobson making it
clear she could not possibly give up her way of life to
return to Hobson.

Is Maggie
bolstering Will
here, or is she
completely serious?

Vickey's entrance interrupts the exchange. She
fulsomely embraces Hobson but recoils at the
suggestion of living with Hobson, which 'her

What are these
circumstances?
circumstances make impossible'. Vickey challenges
Maggie when she tells Hobson he must 'put a collar on'
for Will. 'You're always pretending to folk about your
husband' but Maggie brushes this aside and gives her
ultimatum – 'either I can go home or you can go and
put a collar on for Will'. Hobson is rescued by Alice
who perceives the delicacy of the situation, and Hobson
exits for his collar because 'my neck is cold!'

Maggie is direct with her sisters when she asks 'which
of us is it to be?' Alice is clear she will not break her
home up and Vickey is adamant her 'child comes first'.
Both sisters see that it is Maggie's duty to save Hobson.

Maggie says she must ask Will but neither Vickey nor
Alice countenance such behaviour. Vickey credits Will
as not having 'the spirit of a louse'. Maggie is steady
under the abuse and exits to the shop to meet Will.
Vickey and Alice are glad that returning to live with
Hobson is left to Maggie and Will but they build up to
their fears that Hobson 'might leave them his money'.

Alice decides that Hobson must make his will – drawn
up by Albert, and Vickey is keen to interrupt Maggie
'tutoring' Will in what to say to Hobson. Vickey opens
the door to find Will 'looking over the stock'. Vickey is
indignant at Will's inspection, but he is 'prosperous and
self-confident' and states he needs to know the state of
the business. Will sends Maggie (who takes his hat) to
fetch Hobson and tells her to 'be sharp!' Willie makes it
clear to Alice and Vickey that the business has
degenerated to be worth 'about two-hundred' pounds.
Alice reacts 'Do you mean to tell me father isn't rich?'
Willie outrages Vickey by saying her husband is 'in trade'
and should know the reputation of Hobson's business.

They are horrified to think of Will looking after
Hobson's business and state that Maggie and Will are
simply coming, in Vickey's words, 'to look after father'.

*How does Willie
turn the tables on
Vickey with a lovely
irony?*

Willie makes it clear that 'I'll do the arranging' and
things will be 'on my terms'. Alice tries to assert her
position – 'Will Mossop – do you know who you're
talking to?' Will sums up the conversation with 'we do
get on in the world, don't we?'

Maggie enters with Hobson and Will greets him with a
heavy hand. Hobson has a penitent air with 'I'm a
changed man Will' but we see Will's strategy when he
says 'There used to be room for improvement'. Will
makes it clear that although he is concerned for Hobson,
for Maggie's sake, he will not neglect his own business
for long.

*What do you think
are their motives
for staying?*

When Alice states that she and Vickey want to stay to
see that Hobson is treated fairly, this stings Hobson's
pride. He insists he is easily a match for Will. Hobson
asks both Alice and Vickey directly if they will come to
look after him. Both are forced to say 'No'. Hobson
instructs Will to see Alice and Vickey out and they
leave 'in silent anger' with Vickey giving the final insult,
'Beggars on horseback'. Hobson sums up their attitudes
as having 'necks stiff with pride'.

Hobson makes his 'generous' offer, that Will and
Maggie can 'have the back bedroom for your own',
Maggie can keep house and Will have his old job back
for 'eighteen shillings a week' and share housekeeping
expenses with Hobson. Willie's response is immediate:
'Come home Maggie.' Hobson is dumbfounded,
thinking of Maggie and Will in 'a wretched cellar' in
Oldfield Road. When Hobson dismisses Will, Maggie
tells him that 'if he goes, I go with him, father'. Willie
puts the situation clearly to Hobson. In their year at
Oldfield Road, he and Maggie have paid off Mrs
Hepworth and made money and, at the same time,
taken away Hobson's high-class trade.

Will makes it clear that Hobson's business is being
'starved to death' and yet he has had the audacity to

The truth is about to descend on Hobson.

offer Will eighteen shillings a week to return. Hobson is incredulous and stammers 'but-but-you're Will Mossop, you're my old shoe hand'. Will offers to 'transfer' to Hobson's shop with Hobson having 'half-share on condition you're sleeping partner'. Will astounds Maggie as well as Hobson when he suggests the new name of 'William Mossop, late Hobson'. Maggie calms Hobson's complaints of 'impudence' and refuses to allow 'late Hobson'. Maggie suggests 'Hobson and Mossop'. Will is adamant and prevails with 'Mossop and Hobson'.

Maggie overrides Hobson's retort with 'very well'. Will immediately gives notice of alterations he will make. Hobson's answer is 'in my shop' but we see the new Will with his answer, 'In mine!' Will intends to improve the furniture and to lay carpet. Hobson complains of 'pampering folk' but Will retorts that 'pampering pays'. Hobson is amazed with Will's answer to his challenge, 'Do you think this shop is in Saint Ann's Square, Manchester?' Implacably, Will states, 'It's going to be'. He says that the 'jump' to Saint Ann's Square will be no greater than the jump he has already made.

Will suggests Maggie takes Hobson for 'a bit of fresh air' when he can have the 'deed of partnership' drawn up by Albert Prosser. Hobson is crushed and goes obediently for his hat.

We see the depth of the relationship that Maggie & Will have forged.

Will is amazed at himself – he cannot believe that he has overridden Hobson. He admits that he 'weren't by half so certain as I sounded' but he realises that he is to be 'Master of Hobson's'. Will tells Maggie of his nervousness in challenging her over the shop's name, but Maggie stops him with 'Don't spoil it Will'. She is proud of the way he has taken control.

Will attempts to remove Maggie's brass ring to make 'an improvement' by 'getting you a proper one'. Maggie

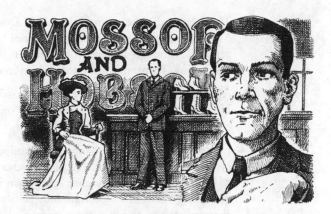

will have none of this. She will wear a gold one 'for show' but will always keep the brass one as a reminder of 'the truth about ourselves'. As Maggie and Will show each other genuine affection Hobson returns and 'meekly' prepares to go to Albert Prosser's.

We feel Will has achieved the unachievable.

The play closes with Will's comment which is pregnant with meaning, 'Well, by gum!'

COMMENT   It is a well-known fact that Hobson's business is ruined. Tubby is happy to discuss openly the reasons with Jim Heeler.

Hobson has failed to realise what is essential to successful selling and has employed the wrong strategies. He has not recognised the competition from Will's business and initially believes that he will be able to dictate terms to Will.

Hobson's breakdown is sudden but suggests his lifestyle must have changed since Maggie has been gone. We see the problems of alcoholism clearly and simply stated. We also see how far Hobson has sunk in the year since Maggie and Will's wedding.

The relationship between Hobson and Doctor MacFarlane is an unusual one but crucial to Hobson's survival. Although Doctor MacFarlane is forthright and controlling, Hobson is attracted to his directness.

Alice and Vickey do not have the compassion toward Hobson that Maggie has; the two show only a selfish concern whereas Maggie tempers Will's conditions.

Like Hobson, Will has changed tremendously in the preceding year; although Maggie has 'schooled' him, he has gained his own confidence and grown in stature. In his management of Hobson he fully achieves his changed stature, to his own amazement. Will has also gained Maggie's ambition and foresight. We also see how Will manages Alice and Vickey.

The relationship between Maggie and Will has deepened and attained an equality.

Although 'saved' Hobson seems defeated and we are left to wonder at his future.

GLOSSARY

Lord Beaconsfield the Prime Minister, Disraeli

cut line less-popular line

toper heavy drinker

ken know

dunderheaded stupid

thraldom enslavery

crack chat

on his mettle wary

worrits worries

over-reached cheated

jibbing complaining

Beggars on horseback upstarts

sleeping partner non-active partner

Identify the speaker.

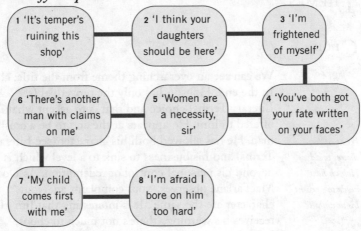

1 'It's temper's ruining this shop'

2 'I think your daughters should be here'

3 'I'm frightened of myself'

6 'There's another man with claims on me'

5 'Women are a necessity, sir'

4 'You've both got your fate written on your faces'

7 'My child comes first with me'

8 'I'm afraid I bore on him too hard'

Check your answers on page 67.

B *Consider these issues.*

a How Hobson has managed the shop since Maggie's departure.

b Why Hobson chose to have Doctor MacFarlane stay in preference to Jim Heeler.

c The way Alice and Vickey have changed since their marriages.

d The reasonableness of Hobson's offer to Maggie and Will.

e The balance of the relationship between Maggie and Will at the end of the play.

f How much of Will's confidence is his own.

g What we are supposed to think about Hobson.

PART THREE

COMMENTARY

THEMES

CHOICE

What earlier choices could Hobson have made to prevent his downfall?

We can see an overarching theme from the title: choice! In the end, Hobson has only the proverbial (see Literary Terms) choice and that is to accept what is offered to him. He appears at the end to be a crushed man. He has allowed both his character (see Literary Terms) and his business to sink to a level which is beyond his personal control or redemption. As Doctor MacFarlane observes, 'your complaint and your character are the same'. It is interesting that Jim Heeler receives his warning, 'there's not much to choose between you. You've both got your fate written on your faces'. Will he choose to curb his visits to Moonraker's?

It is arguable how much 'choice' Willie had in his engagement to Maggie. Certainly he put up little resistance when Ada Figgins was confronted by Maggie, but at that time he may have felt that Maggie was simply his escape route from Ada's mother. In total contradiction to Hobson's predicament however, Will ends the play as master of his own destiny, choosing to buy Maggie a 'proper' ring to seal and, in a sense, consummate their marriage on his terms.

When Hobson needs rescuing, Alice and Vickey choose their new ways of life and leave Maggie and Will to negotiate their new future: perhaps not what they would have chosen, but their sense of duty marks Maggie and Will out from the others.

IMPROVEMENT

'Improvement' is a theme that is important in nineteenth-century literature and would have had much to say to the audiences of Brighouse's day. At the start of the play Willie is 'a natural fool at all else' other than making boots. He has no thought of improving himself and would be 'feared to go' as a bootmaker in one of the 'big shops in Manchester'. Maggie however has 'watched' him for a long time and 'counted on' him for the previous six months. It says much for Maggie's courage that she is prepared so irrevocably to see her future joined with Will's, but she has just been spurred by Hobson's denial of her ever finding a husband, and Harold Brighouse has structured (see Literary Terms) events so that Mrs Hepworth has just praised Will's ability and made him more clearly 'a business idea in the shape of a man'. Willie is 'a treasure' and Maggie has understood this in the literal sense. Without Maggie's ambition, Will would have remained 'a contented slave' with Ada. Maggie has given Will his ''appy dream' and this perhaps gives him the strength to stand up to Hobson.

How important do you feel Mrs Hepworth is in Will's development?

After a month of Maggie's tutoring we learn that Will's 'mind's made up'. He already has his own premises – funded by Mrs Hepworth – and has been 'accepted' by Alice and Vickey. Maggie has given him the ability to make his wedding speech and to talk to Hobson as 'master' of his own household. When we next see Will, a year later, he is 'prosperous and has self-confidence'. He is able to say to Alice 'If we come here, we come here on my terms'. Hobson confesses to Will 'I'm a changed man, Will' but the lovely irony (see Literary Terms) is that Will has changed too – he has made the 'improvement' that he says Hobson needs. Maggie says 'you're the man I made you, and I'm proud', and Will is already thinking of 'the improvements' he is to make at 'Mossop and Hobson's'. Now it is Maggie who has to temper Will's ambition and hold fast to the 'brass ring'.

Will and Maggie have achieved both personal and business 'improvement'. We are left to wonder at Alice's and Vickey's new situation. Certainly they have 'come up in the world' but they have not the compassion showed by Willie and Maggie, and they leave with 'silent anger' as Hobson puts his trust in Will and Maggie, and with lovely symbolism (see Literary Terms) it is Will who is asked to 'open the door for them'.

LOVE

Consider the significance of Maggie's 'brass ring'.

Love and choosing marriage partners are also important themes – connected to the main theme of choice. We are clearly told which couple will be 'thought most of at the Bank' twenty years hence. It is clear that the marriage of Will and Maggie, as well as their bank balance, will be the strongest. It was not a romantic start, but one based on vision and trust. When Alice tells Maggie that 'Courting must come first', the answer is an emphatic 'It needn't'. Our early views of marriage are not encouraging ones. Hobson 'felt grateful for the quiet' when his wife died. He appreciated her only when he felt under the 'dominance of three' (his daughters) and his highest compliment is to describe her as a 'hardy thing'. Later in the play he says of Albert and Freddie 'They're putting chains upon themselves'. Willie is 'tokened' to Ada, not from desire, but from fear of Ada's mother and the 'terrible rough side to her tongue'.

There is no romance here. Alice and Vickey seem to have their share of 'sheep's eyes' but the little we see of their marriage achievements seems not to have improved their natures – they are seen as proud and self-centred.

It is with Will and Maggie that we see a 'higher love'.
Maggie has compared courting with the 'fancy buckle'
as 'All glitter and no use to nobody' but there can be
nothing more romantic than 'I'll wear that ring for ever,
Will'. The love that has grown between Maggie and
Will does not exclude others. There is more than duty
in Maggie's standing up to Will in naming the new
shop. Whereas Hobson has seen marriage as a slavery,
for Will and Maggie it is a freedom and liberation.
Their relationship brings out the best in both of them.
It is a strange marriage which lacked romance at the
start, but it has been built on belief in one another and
matured into a real affection which has been based on
'truth about ourselves'. Will first kissed Maggie to defy
Hobson, but at the very end of the play, he kisses her as
they both celebrate the relationship they have built.

EQUALITY

Hobson is seen as a bullying parent and a bullying
employer. He intends to 'choose a pair of husbands' for
Alice and Vickey since they are 'not even fit to choose
dresses for themselves'. He remembers his wife as a
'handy thing' and clearly had no equality of relationship
with her. Alice and Vickey have challenged Hobson
with their 'bustles' but it is Maggie who champions her
sex. Not only has she the courage to challenge Hobson,
but she also has common sense and ability. Hobson has
dismissed her as 'thirty and shelved' and allows her no
ambition beyond running his shop for her keep.
Hobson has ridiculed the idea of paying his daughters
wages – something which seems to surprise Jim Heeler.
When Mrs Hepworth praises 'a workman to his face'
Hobson is angry. When Maggie suggests it was because
'he deserved it' Hobson is outraged. As he exploits his
daughters who work for no wages, so he exploits his
workmen.

Maggie's challenge to Hobson is in juxtaposition (see Literary Terms) to his denying her the possibility of marriage. In between these events is the visit of Mrs Hepworth and Hobson's 'talk' with Jim Heeler, but when Maggie calls Will from the trap she has said very little. Her mind is made up and she is set on her course. Willie wants to escape but is told 'You'll go back when I've done with you'. Harold Brighouse has reversed the domination role and Maggie is set to gain her liberty and equality, and in doing so, achieve it for Will and her sisters too.

Maggie's strength is not over-powering but enabling.

We see Maggie as being forceful and able, but she does not continue in Hobson's way. Where Hobson's aim has been to subdue and contain his family and workers, Maggie's aim is to improve and liberate. Hobson dismisses Willie as 'a workhouse brat' but Maggie sees him as her 'best chance' to escape the Salford life which is 'too near the bone'. Willie is able to admonish Alice and Vickey a year later with 'we do get on in the world, don't we?' Maggie has claimed not only her own equality but has given her sisters their escape from Hobson and Willie his rise to be his own master. More than this, Maggie achieves a genuine equality with Will in the marriage – both personal and business. They are a real partnership. Harold Brighouse has championed the role of women through Maggie, but in doing so champions a marriage which is seen to be based not only on trust and the hope 'for the best we can get out of it' but on love. Maggie's equality is a real one, not based on dominating but based on enabling. There is nothing harsh or threatening in the Maggie of Act IV. Her equality embraces love and generosity, and that generosity extends to Hobson as she gently supports him at the end. The era of Maggie and Will promises a valuing of people which Hobson could not have understood. It is an era where people can flourish through their abilities and we feel there is no limit to what Maggie and Will can achieve.

PARENTING

The theme of parenting is closely bound with the theme of equality. Both Hobson and Jim Heeler have ruled, or tried to rule, their children with a kind of tyranny. Jim says 'they mostly do as I bid them, and the missus does the leathering if they don't'. Hobson professes he was 'grateful for the quiet when my Mary fell on rest' but bemoans his feeling that now 'my own daughters have got the upper hand of me'. Hobson sums up his daughters' behaviour as 'uppishness' and does not recognise the part they play in making his business successful. The daughters are happy to conspire against him.

Maggie supports both her husband and her father.

In seeing Maggie's management of Will and firm but sympathetic handling of Hobson in Act IV, we can assume that Maggie and Will's 'improvement' will project into parenthood. Vickey has said 'my child comes first' but we must wonder at the Beenstock and Prosser marriages, where Alice and Vickey 'don't need to ask our husbands'. There would seem to be a recipe for conflict. Hobson has exploited Alice and Vickey who have had to employ deceit to obtain their marriages, and in turn they are not prepared to look after Hobson. What may seem a pessimistic view of parenting is cheered at the end when Maggie appears prepared to do more than her 'duty'. Young audiences however will have no difficulty in identifying with Alice and Vickey and their battles with bustles!

ALCOHOLISM

Hobson's downfall is rooted in his alcoholism. Doctor MacFarlane has noted that his complaint and character are inextricably linked. At the outset of the play Hobson needs 'reviving'. It is his drunkenness that has allowed Maggie to trick him into paying the marriage settlements for Vickey and Alice, and he is 'for the Moonraker's' when he has agreed to paying. He cannot recognise his problem, but sees it merely as 'reasonable refreshment' when in fact he is 'drinking himself to death'. At first he tells Maggie 'I can't be an abstainer' but we see hope when he says to Maggie 'I want you now'. He wants to be looked after by Maggie and knows it will entail his teetotalism. He did not, at that point, realise that it would entail his being a 'sleeping partner' with Will having complete control of the business. Harold Brighouse shows us the adverse effects of alcoholism on family life and the ruinous effect it has on business.

The triumph of Maggie and Will

Hobson's Choice is rich in its themes. We see both family and business life. The joy is that Maggie and Will triumph in 'marrying' those aspects of their lives in a loving and successful partnership and they have the compassion to rescue Hobson from his downfall.

Choices have been made. Alice and Vickey have chosen their new situations and circumstances. Will and Maggie will benefit from their move to Hobson's and have set their eyes on Saint Ann's Square. Maggie had not wanted to return to Hobson. She expected 'no holiday existence here with you to keep in health' but we know that Hobson will be treated fairly, and will share in the progress that Will and Maggie will undoubtedly achieve. Maggie has made 'the strongest and finest match a woman's made this fifty year'. Hobson did not 'boast it at the Moonraker's' but

Maggie has predicted correctly. The match is a 'fine' match and both Will and Maggie have grown in stature. They have empowered themselves with choice, and their choices display qualities we can only admire.

STRUCTURE

Harold Brighouse's structuring (see Literary Terms) of the play is skilful and satisfying. Our belief in the characters stems from the carefully structured series of events. Maggie gains the courage to 'claim' Will after Hobson has 'written her off' and Mrs Hepworth has praised Will's abilities. We can feel for Maggie and understand her course of action. Each act has its own satisfying shape with its own convincing development and climax (see Literary Terms).

We learn much from the opening of Act I. Hobson drinks too much and Maggie's strength of will overpowers Albert Prosser. The conflict intensifies when Hobson enters and lectures his daughters on 'uppishness' and then denies Maggie the 'provision' of a husband. When Mrs Hepworth enters we both gain a view of Will and have a glimpse of the source of the 'capital' so necessary to Maggie and Will in Oldfield

Jim Heeler's interaction with Hobson is significant.

Road. Hobson's talk with Jim Heeler hardens his thinking and it is against the background of 'there'll be no weddings here' that Maggie and Will stand up to Hobson. Before this Maggie has wooed the amazed and terrified Will, and dismissed the unfortunate Ada. The climax (see Literary Terms) to the act comes with Hobson's strap and his striking of Will. Willie has started on his road to improvement and Maggie watches him with a pleasure and confidence.

In Act II we see the incompetence of Alice and Vickey and the start of the downward spiral of Hobson. We learn that Hobson is asleep in the warehouse, and the trap can be laid. Willie is 'accepted' by Alice and Vickey with their kisses, and we can contemplate the wedding celebration. Both Albert and Freddie must bow to Maggie's instructions.

Will is growing in stature.

As we see Will bolstered in the eyes and minds of the others, there is the resigned acceptance of Albert with 'I suppose I must'. The satisfying ending sees Will with his 'mind made up' but Maggie still not prepared to trust him with the ring.

Act III starts with Will demonstrating his steady improvement. He only left Hobson's a month before, but he is able to deliver his wedding speech although he is terrified that Albert and Freddie will leave him and Maggie alone. We are prepared for Hobson's visit, and we see the bolstering of Will as 'Master' and Hobson's humbling with the wedding cake. There is a superb sense of theatre when Maggie 'produces' the two couples to amaze Hobson, and in Hobson's angry realisation that he has been 'diddled'. Harold Brighouse has beautifully trapped Hobson in his hatred of lawyers. Hobson's vengeful exit sets the scene for his downfall in Act IV. The act ends on a note of high comedy with Maggie 'claiming' Will and leading him to the bedroom 'by the ear'.

Act IV leads inexorably to the raising of Will over the fallen Hobson. The Doctor's observation that 'women are a necessity' leads into the conflict between Maggie and her two sisters – who will look after Hobson.

Will and Maggie have achieved an enviable equality.

Hobson has the strength to dismiss Alice and Vickey to 'negotiate' with those that 'are willing' to come. Harold Brighouse still has surprises in store as Willie overrides not just Hobson, but Maggie too with his 'Mossop and Hobson'. The development of Maggie and Will is complete and their marriage secure. We can all join in Will's 'Well, by gum!'

HOBSON

At the start of the play Hobson appears to be in control, but he has been to a 'Mason's Meeting' and will 'need reviving'. It is clear that Alice and Vickey are in fear of him, and Albert 'turns to go' when he learns that Hobson is still at home. Hobson is not prepared to accept the 'uppishness' he has noted in the 'rebellious females of this house', and we learn that he hates 'bumptiousness like I hate a lawyer'. He is 'outraged' by his daughters' behaviour and he plans to 'choose husbands' for two of them. His selfishness is seen not only in his denying Maggie a husband, but in the brutal way he speaks to her.

Dominating
Two-faced
Afraid of lawyers
Alcoholic
Looks to Maggie
for salvation

We can only laugh at Hobson when he is so subservient to Mrs Hepworth with his 'You wish to see the identical workman?' and 'very glad to have the honour of serving you', and when she has left he changes to 'last time she puts her foot in my shop'. Hobson will make us laugh, but he appears ridiculous.

We see his meanness when we learn that he pays his daughters no wages and when the mention of 'settlements' means that the marriage plans are 'dead off'. On Hobson's return he is confronted with Maggie's plan to marry Will and his only answer is threat and violence.

When Hobson loses Maggie and Will he completely neglects his business. We can only wonder at Hobson's condition which allowed him to 'fall' into the cellar trap. Maggie has no intention of inviting him to her wedding, but it is to Maggie that he turns for help with his 'sad misfortune'. Hobson is not facing up to his problems. He clutches at Maggie's brief suggestion of a 'counter-action' but is easily made to part with his five hundred pounds.

We see his cynical view of marriage as he leaves Oldfield Road, vowing vengeance on womenfolk as he will 'run that shop with men'. Maggie is certain that Hobson will be 'for the Moonraker's' and when we see him a year later he is suffering from 'chronic alcoholism' and his business is so run-down that his foreman is reduced to keeping house for him.

At this point we warm to him and he gains our sympathy especially when he says to Maggie 'by gum, I want you now'. He has the courage to ask Alice and Vickey to leave and can even ask Will to see them out. When Maggie stands up for him against Will's demands we feel for Hobson and wonder at his future as he meekly goes to Albert Prosser to perform the legalities. Maggie and Will are achieving their dream and we can hope that Hobson will be included in it.

MAGGIE

Maggie shows her strength when she forces Albert to buy his boots and laces when he is courting Alice. She scorns Alice's romantic ideas of courting with her 'fancy buckle' comment. We note her keen comment to Hobson 'How much a week do you give us', but unlike Alice and Vickey, Maggie takes little part in the 'uppishness' argument with Hobson. She is piqued that Hobson is not 'dealing' a husband to her, but she has her plan. We learn that she has 'counted on' Will for six months. We have an inkling of her resourcefulness and determination. She is prepared to brush Ada aside to achieve her ambition, but in doing this she gives Will his ambition and rescues him from a life of 'contented slave', to give him his ''appy dream'.

When Hobson returns, Maggie is 'straight' with him. Unlike Alice and Vickey she does not fear Hobson, and

Steadfast
Unafraid of
Hobson
Ambitious
Caring and
sentimental
Level-headed

states 'I'll have Willie Mossop'. She strikes the right note when she says 'I'm watching you, my lad' – perhaps this carries the right balance between a threat and a statement of confidence. Maggie does not let matters lie but organises her destiny. She tells Freddie to arrange the 'blue paper' with Albert while insisting that her sisters 'accept' Will. However, Maggie does not want Will at all costs, and allows him an escape route – 'If you're not willing, just say so now'. Here is an inkling of Maggie's tender side. Maggie has pursued her ambition for Will in his education and we see the results in the wedding speech.

When Hobson arrives after the wedding Maggie is in control – Hobson must show his acceptance of Will. When Albert threatens to be 'greedy' Maggie quickly resolves the situation. She shows concern not only for her sisters but for Hobson too.

When Maggie returns to Hobson in Act IV it is on Will's terms, but again her concern for Hobson shows and Will must temper his demands. So Maggie shows common sense alongside her ambition, and she has not lost the natural touch that seems to have deserted Vickey and Alice. This sentimental side to Maggie's nature should not be underplayed. We have seen her save one of Mrs Hepworth's flowers to press as a keepsake and we see her great good sense and genuine affection with 'that brass ring stays where you put it'. She says that they 'will not forget the truth' about themselves – Maggie will remain steadfast.

WILLIAM MOSSOP

Humble origins
Gentle
Grows in
confidence
Achieves equality
with Maggie

Willie's opening stage direction describes him as 'not naturally stupid but stunted mentally by a brutalised childhood'. Through the course of the play Will changes and develops tremendously, though he retains a charm and modesty.

When he first appears he is a figure of fun, but Mrs Hepworth has recognised his worth. When Maggie calls him up he knows himself for 'a loyal fool' and knows that Maggie is 'a wonder in the shop'. He says an early 'by gum' at the thought of marrying the 'master's daughter' and we can delight in the realisation and confidence of his 'by gum' that ends the play. Will becomes the strongest man in the play not only because of Maggie, but also because of his latent abilities. He has plain honesty which tells Maggie that he has not 'got the love' and freely admits that he is afraid of Ada's mother. His honesty and courage, as well as Maggie's support enable him to stand up to Hobson. When Hobson visits on his wedding day, Willie has no design in his comments which upset Hobson. He notes the 'satisfaction' folk will gain from Hobson's disgrace, but Hobson misreads Will's intentions. We see his modesty when he reminds Maggie that 'They've a long start on us', and we feel compassion for him when Maggie leads him by the ear to their bedroom.

Will doesn't lose those attributes which make him so likeable. He does not gloat over the defeat of Alice and Vickey or the downfall of Hobson. He is anxious that there is 'no ill-will' between himself and his sisters-in-law and he is worried that he bore 'too hard' on Hobson. He still marvels at his 'own boldness'. Will is full of plans and well on the way to achieving his ambitions, but he retains his gentleness and humility which allow the audience to rejoice with him.

*Alice and
Vickey Hobson*

Alice and Vickey have neither the courage nor the ability of Maggie. Although they have complained about the way Hobson treats them, they are in awe of him. They have made their protests in wearing their bustles but have not achieved any real freedom. They are not free to court openly and we see that both Alice and Albert are terrified that Hobson will discover their meetings. Albert 'turns to go' when he hears that Hobson has not left the house. It is Maggie who helps Albert to sell him his boats, and Maggie who enables Alice to have Albert, and Vickey to have Freddie. It is certain that Alice and Vickey could not have managed this themselves. They cannot 'manage' Hobson and they cannot manage the 'figures' when Maggie has left the shop. They both find it hard to accept Willie. Alice is clear about the 'disgrace' in Maggie marrying him and Vickey holds he 'hasn't the spirit of a louse', but both kiss Will under 'protest', and Maggie can say 'you have approved'. When Alice and Vickey consent to go to Maggie's wedding and wedding-spread, their 'marriage-portions' are assured.

A year later Alice is not prepared to leave her home for Hobson and neither is Vickey now that she is expecting. Their concern is not for Hobson, but for the money they think they might loose. Hobson must 'make his will at once'. Will reminds them of the 'big leg up' he and Maggie gave them when they arranged their marriage-portions. They have to accept being dismissed by Hobson and they leave with bad grace and 'silent anger'. We might wonder if they will accept Maggie's invitation to 'tea-time an a Sunday afternoon' but they have been managed by Maggie this far, and surely Maggie's generosity of spirit will see Hobson's family re-united in the future under a happier regime.

Albert Prosser and Freddie Beenstock   Albert and Freddie are the 'escape routes' for Alice and Vickey to leave Hobson. Albert has been 'courting' Alice, being sure to visit when Hobson is not present. Maggie uses them both to bolster Will in the eyes of her sisters. Freddie is used as the messenger to put the writ on Hobson, while Albert must push furniture through the streets to Oldfield Road. Albert seems intent on exacting as much money from Hobson as possible and Freddie protests at Maggie's moderation. Maggie quells their opposition and through the play they never stand up to her. In Act IV we see that Alice and Vickey 'don't need to ask our husbands' and Will's stature is again increased. Hobson's prediction that Albert and Freddie will 'know what marrying a woman means before long' seems likely to come true.

Mrs Hepworth   Mrs Hepworth shows us a number of points about other characters. She is anxious to track down Willie for his boot-making talents. Through her visit we see Will's present limitations, but also his potential. Hobson is shown up by the way he fawns on Mrs Hepworth, but speaks against her as soon as she is gone. We see Maggie's soft side through the flowers sent by Mrs Hepworth, and it is Mrs Hepworth who has funded Will's new business. Mrs Hepworth's role is small but nevertheless significant.

Jim Heeler   Jim allows us to hear Hobson's thoughts as he seeks advice on marrying off Alice and Vickey. Heeler is in much the same state of health as Hobson – Doctor MacFarlane saw little to choose between them. Heeler seems surprised that Hobson does not pay his daughters, but Heeler's household ultimately relies on 'leathering'. In Act IV Hobson rejects Heeler's counsel in favour of Doctor MacFarlane's.

Ada Figgins	Ada is 'tokened' to Will in Act I before Maggie intervenes. Through her we see the step that Will is taking in marrying Maggie. Ada has seen Will bullied by her mother, and Ada has no ambition. Will would probably have been a 'contented slave' but he is overjoyed that Maggie arranges for him never to return to the Figgins' household.
Doctor MacFarlane	Doctor MacFarlane starkly points out Hobson's illness, 'chronic alcoholism'. His directness appeals to Hobson. The Doctor takes 'a fancy' to Hobson, and Hobson feels he wants to 'teach him a lesson'. Unusually, the Doctor prescribes 'Maggie' together with his 'mixture' and 'total abstinence'. We learn from him that to Hobson alcohol is 'poison … deadly, virulent'. MacFarlane is as direct with Maggie as with Hobson and he leaves happy that Hobson is in 'excellent hands'.
Tubby Wadlow	Tubby is Hobson's faithful foreman. He can follow orders, but cannot make decisions. He can see Hobson's foibles: temper and obstinacy. Tubby is loyal to the point of keeping house for the alcoholic Hobson when 'everybody's call me a doting fool'. Tubby knows that Will and Maggie had been the success of Hobson's but that Maggie has been the greatest loss, 'she's a marvel'. He recognises 'Willie's a good lad' and we must feel his future will be secure under Will's regime.

LANGUAGE & STYLE

Hobson's Choice is a Lancashire play of the Lancashire school (see Literary Terms). The play is not rich in dialect but is firmly in the Lancashire tone (see Literary Terms) of plain speech and straightforwardness. For example, when Albert leaves the shop Maggie says, 'It'll teach him to keep out of here a bit'. Such a comment is wholly conversational in tone and bitingly direct.

The language is powerful and direct, and depends for its power on the expressiveness of the Lancashire accent. Willie is more strongly Lancashire in speech than the other characters. 'I've got wrought up to point' he says, with its strong regional feel. When Maggie raises the possibility of his moving to a city shop he responds 'Nay, I'd be feared to go in them fine places'.

There are some conventions (see Literary Terms) which place the language firmly in Lancashire:

- 'I've nobbut one answer back'
- 'It'll be a grand satisfaction'
- 'I'm feeling awkward, like'

We also have examples of 'owt', 'dost', 'axing' and 'nowty'. Thus the sound of the play is a Lancashire sound, but it is the directness and plain-speaking which lends the language its power. For example, Hobson says 'I'll choose a pair of husbands for you, my girls' and 'if you want the brutal truth, you're past the marrying age'. This directness and forthrightness has the 'tune' of Lancashire people. So much is said economically.

At the end of the play we can rejoice with Will and Maggie with their 'Eh, lad!' and 'Eh, lass!' Their speech is also starkly simple but full of meaning. We hear Will's sincerity in 'Thy pride is not in the same street, lass, with the pride I have in you'. Every word is a monosyllable (see Literary Terms) but there is a profundity and depth to the sense. At the end we can identify and celebrate with Will, not in an elaborate speech, but with his, 'Well, by gum!' – so much meaning in so few words!

PART FOUR

STUDY SKILLS

HOW TO USE QUOTATIONS

One of the secrets of success in writing essays is the way you use quotations. There are five basic principles:

- Put inverted commas at the beginning and end of the quotation
- Write the quotation exactly as it appears in the orginal
- Do not use a quotation that repeats what you have just written
- Use the quotation so that it fits into your sentence
- Keep the quotation as short as possible

Quotations should be used to develop the line of thought in your essays.

Your comment should not duplicate what is in your quotation. For example:

Hobson complains to his daughters about their increase in their uppishness, 'There's been a gradual increase of uppishness towards me'.

Far more effective is to write:

Hobson complains to his daughters about their 'increase in uppishness' towards him.

Always lay out the lines as they appear in the text . For example:

We see how easily Maggie overrides Ada when Maggie says:

'Willie, you wed me.'

Ada: 'It's daylight robbery.'

The most sophisticated way of using the writer's words is to embed them into your sentence:

Hobson makes it clear to his daughters that their 'uppishness' must cease.

When you use quotations in this way, you are demonstating the ability to use text as evidence to support your ideas.

Everyone writes differently. Work through the suggestions given here and adapt the advice to suit your own style and interests. This will improve your essay-writing skills and allow your personal voice to emerge.

The following points indicate in ascending order the skills of essay writing:

- Picking out one or two facts about the story and adding the odd detail
- Writing about the text by retelling the story
- Retelling the story and adding a quotation here and there
- Organising an answer which explains what is happening in the text and giving quotations to support what you write

....

- Writing in such a way as to show that you have thought about the intentions of the writer of the text and that you understand the techniques used
- Writing at some length, giving your viewpoint on the text and commenting by picking out details to support your views
- Looking at the text as a work of art, demonstrating clear critical judgement and explaining to the reader of your essay how the enjoyment of the text is assisted by literary devices, linguistic effects and psychological insights; showing how the text relates to the time when it was written

The dotted line above represents the division between lower and higher level grades. Higher-level performance begins when you start to consider your response as a reader of the text. The highest level is reached when you offer an enthusiastic personal response and show how this piece of literature is a product of its time.

Coursework essay

Set aside an hour or so at the start of your work to plan what you have to do.

- List all the points you feel are needed to cover the task. Collect page references of information and quotations that will support what you have to say. A helpful tool is the highlighter pen: this saves painstaking copying and enables you to target precisely what you want to use.
- Focus on what you consider to be the main points of the essay. Try to sum up your argument in a single sentence, which could be the closing sentence of your essay. Depending on the essay title, it could be a statement about a character: In the final analysis it is Will's generosity of spirit that is his greatest triumph; an opinion about setting: The cellar in Oldfield Road is encouragement for anyone struggling to succeed; or a judgement on a theme: The theme of improvement is relevant and assessible to the audience of today.
- Make a short essay plan. Use the first paragraph to introduce the argument you wish to make. In the following paragraphs develop this argument with details, examples and other possible points of view. Sum up your argument in the last paragraph. Check you have answered the question.
- Write the essay, remembering all the time the central point you are making.
- On completion, go back over what you have written to eliminate careless errors and improve expression. Read it aloud to yourself, or, if you are feeling more confident, to a relative or friend.

If you can, try to type your essay, using a word processor. This will allow you to correct and improve your writing without spoiling its appearance.

Examination essay

The essay written in an examination often carries more marks than the coursework essay even though it is written under considerable time pressure.

In the revision period build up notes on various aspects of the text you are using. Fortunately, in acquiring this set of York Notes on *Hobson's Choice*, you have made a prudent beginning! York Notes are set out to give you vital information and help you to construct your personal overview of the text.

Make notes with appropriate quotations about the key issues of the set text. Go into the examination knowing your text and having a clear set of opinions about it.

In most English Literature examinations you can take in copies of your set books. This is an enormous advantage although it may lull you into a false sense of security. Beware! There is simply not enough time in an examination to read the book from scratch.

In the examination

- Read the question paper carefully and remind yourself what you have to do.
- Look at the questions on your set texts to select the one that most interests you and mentally work out the points you wish to stress.
- Remind yourself of the time available and how you are going to use it.
- Briefly map out a short plan in note form that will keep your writing on track and illustrate the key argument you want to make.
- Then set about writing it.
- When you have finished, check through to eliminate errors.

To summarise, these are the keys to success:

- **Know the text**
- **Have a clear understanding of and opinions on the storyline, characters, setting, themes and writer's concerns**
- **Select the right material**
- **Plan and write a clear response, continually bearing the question in mind**

A typical essay question on *Hobson's Choice* is followed by a sample essay plan in note form. This does not present the only answer to the question, merely one answer. Do not be afraid to include your own ideas, and leave out some of those in the sample! Remember that quotations are essential to prove and illustrate the points you make.

How does the charcter of Willie Mossop develop through the course of the play?

The question anticipates your dealing with the course of events and Will's relationship with other characters. The 'How' of the question asks you to look at underlying reasons and there is scope for your opinion of Will's development.

Here is a possible outline of the answer.

Part 1   The atmosphere in Hobson's at the start of the play; Hobson's complaints to his daughters; Maggie's feelings about marriage conversations; Mrs Hepworth's significance.

Part 2   Our first view of Will – his attitudes and abilities; Maggie's proposal; the role of Ada Figgins – why Will would have stayed with her; the qualities Maggie has seen in Will; Will's attitude to Maggie when Ada has gone – his honesty; Alice's and Vickey's reaction to the news.

Part 3   Hobson's reaction to Maggie's announcement; why does Willie react as he does; what part does Maggie play in this?

Part 4   Will's relationship with Alice and Vickey – how do they show their acceptance of him; Will's growing confidence; what we learn from the scene between

	Willie and Maggie before the wedding – his honèsty and reliability.
Part 5	Will's part in the wedding feast – how he has advanced; his request to Albert and Freddie; his handling of Hobson with lack of subtlety; Maggie's bolstering and management of Will on the wedding night.
Part 6	Will's dealing with Alice and Vickey after Hobson's breakdown – what attitude does he strike with them; Will's bearing down on Hobson – 'there used to be room for improvement'; Will's knowledge of the business and his astute assessment of Hobson's shop; Will's demands and his standing up to Maggie.
Part 7: Conclusion	Will's assessment of himself at the end; he has no ill-will to his sisters-in-law and is concerned that he was too hard on Hobson; Will has achieved a genuine partnership and equality with Maggie; the significance of the rings.

Your considered opinion of Will's progress; he has developed his confidence and risen to importance, but he has retained humility and concern for others.

FURTHER QUESTIONS

Make a plan as shown above and attempt these questions

1 Examine the effects of alcohol in the play. What sympathy can we have for Hobson and his 'chronic alcoholism'?
2 Show what part love and marriage play in *Hobson's Choice*.
3 Describe and examine the differing lives of the women in *Hobson's Choice*.
4 What are the qualities of *Hobson's Choice* that have allowed it to retain its popularity?

PART FIVE

CULTURAL CONNECTIONS

BROADER PERSPECTIVES

The original film version of *Hobson's Choice* starred
Charles Laughton as Hobson. The film is faithful to
the sense of the play and well worth seeing. It adds
credulity to the manner of Hobson finding himself in
the cellar of the corn warehouse.

It would be of interest to compare the themes of
Hobson's Choice with some of the following:

- *The History of Mr Polly* by H.G. Wells (Everyman,
  1910). Mr Polly is the archetype of 'life begins at
  forty'. After suffering fifteen years in a poor marriage
  and with a failing business he finds a new and happy
  life. His escape route starts with a fake suicide.
- *Arms and the Man* by George Bernard Shaw
  (Longman, 1898). We see the higher love achieved by
  Raina and Bluntschli which can be profitably
  compared with the love between Maggie and Will.
  We also see Louka's ambition and striving to achieve
  equality.
- *Hindle Wakes* by Stanley Houghton (Heinemann,
  1912). Houghton was, like Harold Brighouse, a
  member of the Manchester School (see Literary
  Terms). *Hindle Wakes* is firmly a Lancashire play
  where the working-class Fanny Hawthorn defies her
  parents, and the conventions of the day, by refusing to
  marry her seducer, the rich son of her father's old
  friend and employer. Like Maggie, Fanny is very
  much in control of her destiny.
- *Spring and Port Wine* by Bill Naughton (Heinemann,
  1965). This play shows us a tyrannical father, Rafe,
  who faces rebellion from his children. Unlike Hobson
  however, Rafe is able to retrieve the situation himself.

character qualities and behaviour of people in literary works

climax highpoint in the development of events

conventions common features e.g. of Lancashire dialect

development stages in the action of a play/literary work

dialect version of speech found in one particular area or region

image a comparison or word/picture to strengthen meaning

irony a seeming contradiction

juxtaposition placing one thing next to another for effect

Lancashire School a group of writers (see Harold Brighouse's Background) associated with the Gaiety Theatre. Stanley Houghton (*Hindle Wakes*) and Allen Monkhouse (*The Conquering Hero*)

are other well-known authors of the school

Manchester School see Lancashire School

monosyllable words with only one syllable

muse writer's inspiration (after nine Greek Goddesses who inspired the Arts)

proverbial as embodied in particular sayings. In this case Hobson has 'Hobson's Choice', meaning, as in the proverb, no choice at all

structure the way the plot is shaped

symbolism something which represents something else of importance

theme the essential ideas in a work

tone atmosphere created by choice of words

universality having relevance to people of all generations

TEST ANSWERS

TEST YOURSELF (Act I)

A 1 Albert Prosser
••• 2 Hobson
3 Vickey
4 Maggie
5 Willie
6 Jim Heeler
7 Maggie
8 Ada

TEST YOURSELF (Act II)

A 1 Tubby
••• 2 Alice
3 Freddie
4 Willie
5 Alice
6 Vickey
7 Maggie
8 Albert

TEST YOURSELF (Act III)

A 1 Willie
••• 2 Maggie
3 Freddie
4 Albert
5 Hobson
6 Maggie
7 Willie
8 Hobson

TEST YOURSELF (Act IV)

A 1 Tubby
••• 2 Jim Heeler
3 Hobson
4 Doctor MacFarlane
5 Doctor MacFarlane
6 Maggie
7 Vickey
8 Willie

NOTES

NOTES

NOTES

NOTES

NOTES

GCSE and equivalent levels (£3.50 each)

Harold Brighouse
Hobson's Choice

Charles Dickens
Great Expectations

Charles Dickens
Hard Times

George Eliot
Silas Marner

William Golding
Lord of the Flies

Thomas Hardy
The Mayor of Casterbridge

Susan Hill
I'm the King of the Castle

Barry Hines
A Kestrel for a Knave

Harper Lee
To Kill a Mockingbird

Arthur Miller
A View from the Bridge

Arthur Miller
The Crucible

George Orwell
Animal Farm

J.B. Priestley
An Inspector Calls

J.D. Salinger
The Catcher in the Rye

William Shakespeare
Macbeth

William Shakespeare
The Merchant of Venice

William Shakespeare
Romeo and Juliet

William Shakespeare
Twelfth Night

George Bernard Shaw
Pygmalion

John Steinbeck
Of Mice and Men

Mildred D. Taylor
Roll of Thunder, Hear My Cry

James Watson
Talking in Whispers

A Choice of Poets

Nineteenth Century Short Stories

Poetry of the First World War

Advanced level (£3.99 each)

Margaret Atwood
The Handmaid's Tale

Jane Austen
Emma

Jane Austen
Pride and Prejudice

William Blake
Poems/Songs of Innocence and Songs of Experience

Emily Brontë
Wuthering Heights

Geoffrey Chaucer
Wife of Bath's Prologue and Tale

Joseph Conrad
Heart of Darkness

Charles Dickens
Great Expectations

F. Scott Fitzgerald
The Great Gatsby

Thomas Hardy
Tess of the D'Urbervilles

Seamus Heaney
Selected Poems

James Joyce
Dubliners

William Shakespeare
Antony and Cleopatra

William Shakespeare
Hamlet

William Shakespeare
King Lear

William Shakespeare
Macbeth

William Shakespeare
Othello

Mary Shelley
Frankenstein

Alice Walker
The Color Purple

John Webster
The Duchess of Malfi

FUTURE TITLES IN THE YORK NOTES SERIES

Chinua Achebe
Things Fall Apart

Edward Albee
Who's Afraid of Virginia Woolf?

Jane Austen
Mansfield Park

Jane Austen
Northanger Abbey

Jane Austen
Persuasion

Jane Austen
Sense and Sensibility

Samuel Beckett
Waiting for Godot

John Betjeman
Selected Poems

Robert Bolt
A Man for All Seasons

Charlotte Brontë
Jane Eyre

Robert Burns
Selected Poems

Lord Byron
Selected Poems

Geoffrey Chaucer
The Franklin's Tale

Geoffrey Chaucer
The Knight's Tale

Geoffrey Chaucer
The Merchant's Tale

Geoffrey Chaucer
The Miller's Tale

Geoffrey Chaucer
The Nun's Priest's Tale

Geoffrey Chaucer
The Pardoner's Tale

Geoffrey Chaucer
Prologue to the Canterbury Tales

Samuel Taylor Coleridge
Selected Poems

Daniel Defoe
Moll Flanders

Daniel Defoe
Robinson Crusoe

Shelagh Delaney
A Taste of Honey

Charles Dickens
Bleak House

Charles Dickens
David Copperfield

Charles Dickens
Oliver Twist

Emily Dickinson
Selected Poems

John Donne
Selected Poems

Douglas Dunn
Selected Poems

George Eliot
Middlemarch

George Eliot
The Mill on the Floss

T.S. Eliot
The Waste Land

T.S. Eliot
Selected Poems

Henry Fielding
Joseph Andrews

E.M. Forster
Howards End

E.M. Forster
A Passage to India

John Fowles
The French Lieutenant's Woman

Elizabeth Gaskell
North and South

Oliver Goldsmith
She Stoops to Conquer

Graham Greene
Brighton Rock

Graham Greene
The Heart of the Matter

Graham Greene
The Power and the Glory

Thomas Hardy
Far from the Madding Crowd

Thomas Hardy
Jude the Obscure

Thomas Hardy
The Return of the Native

Thomas Hardy
Selected Poems

L.P. Hartley
The Go-Between

Nathaniel Hawthorne
The Scarlet Letter

Ernest Hemingway
A Farewell to Arms

Ernest Hemingway
The Old Man and the Sea

Homer
The Iliad

Homer
The Odyssey

Gerard Manley Hopkins
Selected Poems

Ted Hughes
Selected Poems

Aldous Huxley
Brave New World

Henry James
Portrait of a Lady

Ben Jonson
The Alchemist

Ben Jonson
Volpone

James Joyce
A Portrait of the Artist as a Young Man

John Keats
Selected Poems

Philip Larkin
Selected Poems

D.H. Lawrence
The Rainbow

D.H. Lawrence
Selected Stories

D.H. Lawrence
Sons and Lovers

D.H. Lawrence
Women in Love

Laurie Lee
Cider with Rosie

Christopher Marlowe
Doctor Faustus

Arthur Miller
Death of a Salesman

John Milton
Paradise Lost Bks I & II

John Milton
Paradise Lost IV & IX

Sean O'Casey
Juno and the Paycock

George Orwell
Nineteen Eighty-four

John Osborne
Look Back in Anger

Wilfred Owen
Selected Poems

Harold Pinter
The Caretaker

Sylvia Plath
Selected Works

Alexander Pope
Selected Poems

Jean Rhys
Wide Sargasso Sea

William Shakespeare
As You Like It

William Shakespeare
Coriolanus

William Shakespeare
Henry IV Pt 1

William Shakespeare
Henry IV Pt II

William Shakespeare
Henry V

William Shakespeare
Julius Caesar

William Shakespeare
Measure for Measure

William Shakespeare
Much Ado About Nothing

William Shakespeare
A Midsummer Night's Dream

William Shakespeare
Richard II

William Shakespeare
Richard III

William Shakespeare
Sonnets

William Shakespeare
The Taming of the Shrew

William Shakespeare
The Tempest

William Shakespeare
The Winter's Tale

George Bernard Shaw
Arms and the Man

George Bernard Shaw
Saint Joan

Richard Brinsley Sheridan
The Rivals

R.C. Sherriff
Journey's End

Muriel Spark
The Prime of Miss Jean Brodie

John Steinbeck
The Grapes of Wrath

John Steinbeck
The Pearl

Tom Stoppard
Rosencrantz and Guildenstern are Dead

Jonathan Swift
Gulliver's Travels

John Millington Synge
The Playboy of the Western World

W.M. Thackeray
Vanity Fair

Mark Twain
Huckleberry Finn

Virgil
The Aeneid

Derek Walcott
Selected Poems

Oscar Wilde
The Importance of Being Earnest

Tennessee Williams
Cat on a Hot Tin Roof

Tennessee Williams
The Glass Menagerie

Tennessee Williams
A Streetcar Named Desire

Virginia Woolf
Mrs Dalloway

Virginia Woolf
To the Lighthouse

William Wordsworth
Selected Poems

W.B. Yeats
Selected Poems

York Notes – the Ultimate Literature Guides

York Notes are recognised as the best literature study guides.
If you have enjoyed using this book and have found it useful, you
can now order others directly from us – simply follow the ordering
instructions below.

HOW TO ORDER

Decide which title(s) you require and then order in one of the following
ways:

Booksellers
All titles available from good bookstores.

By post
List the title(s) you require in the space provided overleaf,
select your method of payment, complete your name and
address details and return your completed order form and
payment to:

> *Addison Wesley Longman Ltd*
> *PO BOX 88*
> *Harlow*
> *Essex CM19 5SR*

By phone
Call our Customer Information Centre on 01279 623923 to
place your order, quoting mail number: HEYN1.

By fax
Complete the order form overleaf, ensuring you fill in your
name and address details and method of payment, and fax it
to us on 01279 414130.

By e-mail
E-mail your order to us on awlhe.orders@awl.co.uk listing
title(s) and quantity required and providing full name and
address details as requested overleaf. Please
quote mail number: HEYN1. Please do not
send credit card details by e-mail.

York Notes Order Form

Titles required:

Quantity	Title/ISBN	Price

Sub total _____

Please add £2.50 postage & packing _____

(*P & P is free for orders over £50*) _____

Total _____

Mail no: HEYN1

Your Name _____

Your Address _____

_____

Postcode _____ Telephone _____

Method of payment

☐ I enclose a cheque or a P/O for £_____ made payable to Addison Wesley Longman Ltd

☐ Please charge my Visa/Access/AMEX/Diners Club card
Number _____ Expiry Date _____
Signature _____ Date _____

(please ensure that the address given above is the same as for your credit card)

Prices and other details are correct at time of going to press but may change without notice. All orders are subject to status.

☐ *Please tick this box if you would like a complete listing of Longman Study Guides (suitable for GCSE and A-level students)*

York Press

Longman

Addison Wesley Longman